Beauty and the Beast

RETOLD BY

D E L L A   R O W L A N D

ILLUSTRATED BY

B A R B A R A   L A N Z A

A CALICO BOOK

Published by Contemporary Books, Inc.

CHICAGO · NEW YORK

Rowland, Della.
Beauty and the beast / Della Rowland.
p.   cm.
Summary: Through her great capacity to love, a kind and beautiful
maid releases a handsome prince from the spell which has made him an
ugly beast.
ISBN 0-8092-4304-0
[1. Fairy tales.   2. Folklore.]   I. Title.
PZ8.R792Be   1990
389.2—dc20   89-22326
                                                               CIP
                                                               AC

For my mother,
Florence Whitlow Simpson,
who loved me for myself
—DR

For my
mother and father
—BL

Published by Contemporary Books, Inc.
180 North Michigan Avenue, Chicago, Illinois 60601
Manufactured in the United States of America
Library of Congress Catalog Card Number: 89-22326
International Standard Book Number: 0-8092-4304-0

Published simultaneously in Canada by Beaverbooks, Ltd.
195 Allstate Parkway, Valleywood Business Park
Markham, Ontario L3R 4T8 Canada

Once upon a time, in a prosperous seaport, there lived a rich shipping merchant. His wife had died years before, leaving him three sons and three daughters who were his heart's delight. But it was the youngest daughter who was his favorite. Because she had a heart that was as kind as her face was lovely, she had always been called the beautiful child—or Beauty.

Now the merchant, being sensible as well as rich, spared no expense on his children's education. All six had the finest tutors in music, languages, and literature. When they were grown up, the three sons decided to help their father improve his business. The merchant's two eldest daughters preferred to improve their lot by trying to attract rich husbands. By day they strolled about the parks showing off their fashionable clothes, and at night they attended grand balls or the theater in order to meet gentlemen who would be good enough for them. Beauty, who had never lost her love for learning, spent her days reading. In the evenings she played her father's favorite songs for him on her harpsichord. She had many suitors, but she told them all she was not yet ready to leave her father.

Life can change suddenly, sometimes for the worse. One summer, every single one of the merchant's ships sank in a terrible storm and all his goods were lost at sea. His business was ruined. All his wealth was gone. He had to sell his fine home and all his possessions—all but a small cottage in the country, far away from the city. He sadly told his children that they must now move to this cottage, where, with hard work, they could grow enough food to feed themselves.

His two eldest daughters were shocked! Leave the city? "We don't know any other way to live," they pleaded. Grow their own food? "This is outrageous!" they stormed. The solution for them was clear. "We have suitors begging us to marry them," they said proudly. "We'll simply have to decide which ones to accept."

Unfortunately, they were embarrassed to discover
that their so-called admirers wanted nothing to do
with them now that they were poor. So the
sisters had no choice but to go to the country with
their family. The truth was, their neighbors were
glad to see the sisters become poor because
they were so snobby and pompous. "Let them
stroll about in their fancy gowns and impress
the sheep," the townspeople laughed.

Beauty and her brothers felt great pity for their father in his misfortune and never uttered one complaint about moving. As soon as they had settled into their country house, the sons began planting potatoes, cabbages, tomatoes, beans, and sweet peppers. Beauty discovered that she had to rise at four o'clock every morning in order to clean the house, wash the family's clothes, and cook the meals. When their clothing began to wear out, she taught herself how to sew. At first, she fell into bed every night exhausted. But gradually the hard work made her stronger. And as she learned how to grow vegetables and herbs, she took great delight in watching the tiny green shoots poke up through the soft, warm earth. She began to realize that all education and enjoyment in life did not come just from books and travel.

Her sisters were no help to her. They burned the stew and tore the laundry and were horrified at the blisters they got when they tried to sweep the floor. Finally they became so unhappy and bitter about their new life that they stopped even trying to help. Mostly, they were bored to tears. They rose at ten o'clock and spent their days strolling around, trying to ignore the chickens pecking in the yard. They complained about no longer having fine clothes to wear and whined about being unable to attend any more fancy parties. They simply couldn't understand why Beauty was so content to live in this lonely cottage.

One day, word came to the merchant that one of his ships had been found. "I should go to the seaport at once to claim some of our lost fortune," he told his family.

"Father, is it true?" the eldest daughters cried. "Are we rich again? Now we can move back to the city! You must bring us back some suitable dresses. And we'll need hats and jewelry too."

"And what shall I bring you, Beauty?" asked her father. Beauty thought to herself that whatever money her father might recover would never be enough to buy all this.

"A rose," she replied. "I have not seen one since we moved."

So the merchant set off for the city with high hopes. The trip took him through a great forest. Riding through the dense woods, he thought he smelled the heavy fragrance of roses. "I've never seen a rose in these woods," he thought. In an instant, the smell was gone. "My nose must be getting older than the rest of me," he said, laughing out loud.

When he arrived at the seaport, he received only bad news. His goods had been seized by lawyers to pay his debts. Nothing was left for him. So, after all his hopes, the merchant started back again, as poor as when he arrived.

On his way home a terrible ice storm blew up in the great forest. The air was white with snow. In a matter of minutes, the road through the trees disappeared in the blinding swirls. The merchant knew he was lost. His horse stumbled against the fierce, driving wind and threw him to the ground. The merchant then plodded along on foot, pulling the horse by the reins behind him. Soon night fell, and he could hear wolves howling. "I must keep walking," he thought desperately, "or I'm bound to freeze to death or be eaten."

Through the thick snowfall, he saw a dim light in the distance. "Someone must live nearby," he thought, "a woodcutter, perhaps." Stumbling forward, he found himself beneath a long row of huge trees whose tops formed an arch above his head. Here the wind was strangely still and the blizzard was only a gentle snowfall. This queer sight made the merchant uneasy, but the possibility of safety spurred him on.

He thought he was dreaming when he found himself before a huge castle! "How odd," he said as he entered the gates. "The courtyards are all lit up, but there are no servants around." His horse trotted eagerly into the open stable door where it smelled oats and fresh hay in an empty stall. When the merchant tied up his horse, he was puzzled to find no other horses there.

Entering the castle, the merchant found himself in a large room as empty and silent as the courtyard. In front of a blazing fire stretched a long table set for one person. It was loaded with gold platters of beef and turkey, tureens of steaming soup, and baskets of cakes and ripe fruit. The merchant sat down by the fire to dry himself and politely waited for his host to come down to dinner. "Surely the master of this magnificent castle won't mind if I warm myself by his fire," the merchant thought. "He should be down soon, for his supper is ready."

Eleven o'clock struck, and still no one had come. Finally, the hungry merchant couldn't resist the meat and cakes that smelled so inviting. Timidly, he took a turkey leg and a swallow of wine. He was so hungry and there was so much food that he couldn't help but gobble down more.

Feeling refreshed and a bit bolder, he wandered down a hallway until he came to an open door. Inside the room was a bed all turned down. The merchant crawled in and immediately fell asleep.

It was late the next morning when he woke. On a chair next to his bed was a new suit of clothes, made of velvet and exactly his size. "How kind my host is to me!" he exclaimed. "I wish he would show me his face, so I could thank him." Out on the long table where he had eaten the night before were eggs and meat and a steaming cup of cocoa. This time, the merchant knew the meal was meant for him and he sat right down to eat.

When the merchant stepped out into the courtyard to
fetch his horse, he was astonished to find the snow had
vanished. Before his eyes were rows and rows of fragrant
roses—yellow, pink, crimson, and white. "These must have
been the roses I smelled on my way to the seaport. How
could I have missed them last night?" he wondered in
amazement. "Well, even if I have nothing for the others at
least I can bring Beauty her rose."

Just as he plucked the most perfect yellow bud, the
bushes parted and an animal, walking upright and dressed in
a man's clothing, lunged toward him.

"You ungrateful man!" the beast hissed. "I saved your life and this is how you repay me—by stealing my roses! These flowers mean more to me than anything. They are all the beauty I possess. You shall pay for that one bud with your life!"

The poor merchant was so terrified that his knees buckled beneath him. "Oh, sir, forgive me, please!" he cried. "I never intended to offend such a kind host. There were so many roses, I didn't dream you'd miss just one. It's the only thing my dearest daughter wished me to bring her."

"Don't call me 'sir' again!" the beast roared. "I hate lies. I detest flattery. Speak the plain truth to me. I am the Beast. That is what I am, and that is what I am called."

The Beast paused, then pointed a claw at the trembling man. "I may forgive you on one condition. If it was for your daughter you plucked one of my roses, then your daughter must die in your place. She must come of her own free will, and if she refuses to come, you must return in three months. Don't think you can hide from me. If you do not come back, I'll find you wherever you are."

Well, the merchant had no intention of sending Beauty to be eaten by this monster. But he agreed to the Beast's condition so that he could have a little time with his family before he died.

"Good," replied the Beast. "Now before you go, return to your bedroom. You will find an empty chest. Fill it to the top with whatever you want, and it will be at your home when you arrive. I am still your host, and I won't have you leave my home empty-handed. Now be gone!" And, with that, the Beast disappeared into the bushes.

With a heavy heart, the merchant did as he was told. In his bedroom he found the chest, as well as piles of gold coins and jewels. But he could hardly see what he put in the chest through the tears in his eyes. "At least my children will have some money to live on after I am dead," he thought miserably. Finally he saddled up his horse and set out for home.

The horse seemed to know its own way home through the dense trees. In a short time, the merchant rode through the gates of his own little house. He told his children his sad tale, then handed Beauty her rose. "Here, my Beauty, is your rose. I'm afraid it has cost me dearly."

"You silly girl!" shrieked the middle daughter. "See what trouble your stupid rose has caused our father? Who will take care of us now?"

Taking her father's hand, Beauty said calmly, "Father will not die because of me. The Beast has asked for me to return, and I shall be the one to go to the castle to face his fury."

"No, sister," said her brothers. "You shall not die! We'll find this monster and kill him, then we'll all be safe."

"Alas," said their father, shaking his head, "this Beast's powers are so great that there is no escaping him. Beauty, I could never let you die for me. You are young, with your whole life ahead of you. I'm an old man. I don't have many years left."

"I would rather be eaten myself than die of grief at having caused your death," Beauty told her father firmly. Her father and brothers pleaded and protested, but Beauty was determined to go.

That night when the merchant went to bed, he found that the chest of gold had miraculously appeared in his room. He told only his sons and Beauty about it, for he was afraid his other daughters would want to move back to the city and squander it. But Beauty told him that two young men who lived nearby had come courting her sisters. She urged her father to use some of the money for their dowries so that they might marry, which they were eager to do.

And so Beauty's two sisters were both married, and the family was happy for a while. But all too soon the three months were over, and Beauty and her father grimly set out for the dreaded Beast's castle.

It was evening when Beauty and the merchant reached the castle. Just as before, the courtyard was all lit up and empty. As if it had always lived there, the horse went by itself into the stable and began eating.

This time the long dining table was set for two people. Beauty and her father sat down, but they were too nervous to eat a bite. Suddenly, the Beast appeared from behind a curtained doorway. Even though he had entered the room as quietly as a mouse, his animal face was so terrifying to Beauty that it seemed to roar at her! She tried to appear calm, even though she was trembling violently.

The Beast stared at Beauty with glittering gold eyes. Finally he asked, "Have you come of your own free will?"

"I . . . I have," Beauty answered in a small voice.

The Beast's eyes turned a gentle green. "Then you are as kind as you are beautiful," he said. "I am grateful to you." Then, turning to Beauty's father, he said, "Tomorrow morning you must leave, good man, and never think of returning to this castle. Good night, then." He turned and was gone so quickly and silently that the curtains hardly swayed as he passed through the door.

Neither Beauty nor her father thought they would be able to close their eyes that night. But no sooner had their heads touched their pillows than they were fast asleep.

That night Beauty had a dream in which a woman told her that she had nothing to fear and that her sacrifice for her father would be rewarded. When Beauty woke the next morning, she hurried to tell her father of her dream, hoping it would comfort him. But, in spite of the dream, her father wept bitterly as the time approached for him to leave his daughter.

"I won't go!" he cried. "I won't leave you to this horrible fate!"

"You must go, Father," she insisted bravely. "Let's trust that my dream is a good sign." After he had gone, she leaned against the castle wall and sobbed. She didn't know which was worse: seeing her father so heartbroken or knowing she would soon die in the jaws of an awful monster.

But Beauty was a brave young woman, and after a while she decided that if today was her last day to live she wouldn't spend it weeping. So she set out to explore the castle.

It was a splendid castle, indeed. Great hallways with massive doors led to rooms filled with all her favorite books, intricately woven tapestries, games, and every musical instrument that existed. At last she came to a door with these words written above it: BEAUTY'S ROOM.

The doors swung open by themselves. Inside was a swan-shaped bed with a coverlet made of pure-white swan feathers. Elegant gowns filled the closet, and necklaces made of rare jewels covered the dresser. To her delight, there was also a harpsichord! A window overlooked the rose garden.

"Why would the Beast go to all this trouble to create a special room for me if he intends to kill me tonight?" she wondered aloud.

She took down a book from the shelf and opened it. These words were written in golden letters on the page: *All your wishes will be granted.*

Beauty's eyes filled with tears. "All I wish for is to see my father again," she cried.

Instantly, in a mirror on the wall, she saw her father riding through the gate at their cottage and being greeted by her sisters and brothers. Then the vision faded, leaving only

the reflection of her tearstained face. Beauty was relieved to
see her father was safely home. "The Beast must have some
kindness in his heart to show me this comforting scene," she
said to herself. Feeling better, she sat down to play her
father's favorite song on the harpsichord.

At noon, she listened to the music of a lute being played while she ate, although she saw no musicians. Then she spent the rest of the afternoon exploring other rooms and wandering about the rose garden. That evening, the long table was set for one. As she sat down to her supper, the curtains rustled and the Beast appeared again, staring at her. Beauty sat stiffly at the table, terrified.

"Beauty, may I join you while you eat your meal?" the Beast asked.

She was surprised that his voice was so soft. "Of course, Beast," she whispered, although she thought she wouldn't be able to eat with him so close and watching her. "You are the master here. You may do whatever you like."

"Oh, no," replied the Beast. "You are the one who rules this castle. You have only to tell me to leave and I will go. I'll understand. I know I am monstrous to look at. Tell me, am I not ugly to you?"

Beauty was afraid that her answer would make him angry. "I cannot lie to you," she answered, "but I think you must be very kind. Many men who are handsome in the face have monstrous hearts. To me a kind heart is more important."

"It is you who have the kind heart, Beauty," sighed the Beast. "Not only am I monstrous to look at, but I am not very interesting to talk to," he lamented.

"But I have seen your rooms full of books and musical instruments and paintings," replied Beauty. "You cannot be dull and still love these things as you do."

"Thank you, Beauty," said the Beast. "I will leave you now. If you permit me I will meet you again tomorrow evening at nine o'clock. Amuse yourself, for everything in the castle is yours. I would be miserable if you were unhappy. There is only one promise you must make to me; you must never try to find me during the day in the woods beyond the castle wall—and never ask me why."

Beauty promised without any question. By now she had lost almost all her fear of him. But when the Beast rose to retire, she was startled when he gripped the table with his paw and asked. "Beauty, would you be my wife?"

Terror seized her once more. Finally she answered, "Beast, forgive me, but I cannot do that." The Beast was strangely silent. Beauty was shocked to see that his eyes were full of longing and pain rather than anger. He looked at her for a moment longer, then let out a sad, low moan.

"Farewell then, my Beauty," he whispered and left the great room. When she was alone again, Beauty stopped shaking. She felt pity for the Beast's sadness, but she could not bear the thought of being his wife.

Soon three months had passed since Beauty had come to live in the castle. She spent her days reading, weaving, and playing music. Each night, the Beast joined her at nine o'clock and they talked about music or magic or her family or his precious roses. And each night, just before he left, he asked Beauty to marry him. She refused him every time, and every time he became sadder and sadder.

Still, she no longer dreaded seeing him. In fact, as nine o'clock approached, she found herself glancing at the door, eager for his appearance. Even though she had everything she wanted during the day, it was not enough, for she was lonely when she was not with the Beast.

Sometimes they walked in the rose garden or the courtyard. Once she asked him if he would show her a stream that she could hear gurgling in the woods beyond the courtyard. The Beast became tense, and his eyes glittered gold. He was quiet for a moment before answering her.

"Oh, Beauty, I told you once never to follow me into the woods. You can never go to the stream with me, for deer and other small animals who live in the forest come there to drink. When I am near them, I . . . I cannot help myself . . . I am a beast, after all, and a beast must eat . . ."

"Oh, stop! Stop!" she cried. Horrified, Beauty could not bear to hear any more, and she ran away from him. How could her Beast, who was so tender and careful with her, commit such terrible acts? After a while, however, she realized how ashamed he had been to tell her this awful truth. Her heart broke to think of him so humiliated.

The next evening at nine o'clock, she was relieved to see him draw back the heavy curtain to the dining room. She rushed up to him.

"Oh, Beast," she exclaimed. "I was afraid you might not come tonight. I'm so sorry I ran away last night. I was childish and rude."

"I don't blame you for being horrified, Beauty," the Beast said gently. "We need not speak of it again."

At the end of the evening, the Beast once again asked Beauty if she would be his wife.

"Oh, Beast, I wish I could marry you," Beauty replied. "It distresses me to see you so sad each time I refuse you. I've grown very fond of you since I came to the castle, but I must be honest. I can never marry you, but I will stay here with you. Can you be content with my friendship, which I give freely and forever?"

"I suppose I must," whispered the Beast. Then, as he did every night, the Beast sighed a mournful sigh and said, "Farewell then, my Beauty."

The next day Beauty saw an alarming vision of her father in the magic mirror. He had become sick over losing her and was near death. Beauty could do nothing but weep the whole day. That evening she told the Beast what she had seen and begged him to let her visit her poor father. "I only want to assure him that I am happy," she pleaded. The Beast's eyes filled with fear as he listened to her.

"I'll send you to your father tomorrow," he said. "But I know you will stay with him, and then it will be your Beast who dies of sorrow."

"No, no," Beauty cried, "I could never go if it would hurt you. It's just that my father is alone now. My sisters married and moved to the city, and the magic mirror showed me that my brothers have joined the king's soldiers. Let me go for one week. I promise to return."

"Very well," said the Beast. "When you wake up tomorrow morning, you will be there. You have only to take off this ring when you wish to come back to me. Farewell then, my Beauty. Don't forget your promise to me."

Sure enough, the next
morning, Beauty woke up in
her father's house. She ran
to his room immediately to
show him she was not only alive
but also happy. Just the sight of his
favorite daughter enabled him to get
up from his bed and eat the
heartiest breakfast he'd had in months.

Beauty's sisters were sent for
immediately. When they arrived with their
husbands, Beauty could tell that her
sisters were miserable. One had married an
extremely handsome man. But he was so
vain he couldn't pay any attention to
anyone but himself. The other sister had
married a very clever, witty man.
Unfortunately, he used his wit only to
insult everyone, especially his wife.

"How odd," Beauty thought to herself. "My sisters' husbands have the two qualities most sought after in a man—good looks and wit. But neither good looks nor wit has made these men kind fellows or good company." She felt sorry for her sisters now because what they had sought had not made them happy. It seemed to Beauty that they had looked only for the qualities and not seen the real men.

Oh, how she missed her Beast! How happy she was when she was with him! She realized how much she had come to appreciate him, in spite of his looks. She loved his honesty and tenderness and the great respect he always gave her. Her heart ached for her sisters. She wished they could each have as wonderful a companion as her Beast.

Too soon, the week was up and it was time for Beauty to return to the castle. But she was so glad to be with her father, who was getting stronger all the time, that she stayed one more day, then another. On the tenth night, she saw a vision in her mirror as she was combing her hair. The Beast was lying beside a stream, nearly dead and clutching a single white rose in his paw. His beautiful eyes looked at her, full of suffering. She burst into tears!

"My promise!" she sobbed. "How could I break my promise to the Beast? He has shown me nothing but kindness and love. Why *shouldn't* I marry him? I would be happier than my sisters are with their husbands. Even if I don't love him, I admire and respect him, and I would always be cherished and honored by him. He would die to make me happy! Oh, dear! What if he has died already, thinking that I am happier here with my family than with him?"

With that, Beauty lay her ring on the table next to her bed and at once was fast asleep. To her relief, she woke the next morning in the castle. She was impatient the whole day. She didn't know where the Beast spent his days, and she was afraid to venture out into the woods for fear of seeing him feasting on a gentle deer. But when the clock struck nine, and no Beast appeared, she became frantic thinking he might be dead.

Blindly, she ran into the woods calling his name. It no longer mattered to her what horrible act she might see him doing there. She remembered that in her vision the Beast was lying beside a stream. She followed the sound of gurgling water until she stumbled over her Beast. He was lying on the ground, as still as a stone.

"What have I done?" she cried. "The Beast is dead!"
Heartbroken, she threw herself down and lay her head on
his chest, shaking with sobs. It was then she felt his heart
beating faintly. Quickly she cupped some water from the
stream in her hands, gently patted it on his face, and called
his name softly.

The Beast slowly opened his eyes. "You forgot your
promise," he whispered hoarsely. "I felt such grief when you
left that I resolved to die of hunger. I die content, however,
now that you are near again.

"Oh, no, my Beast," cried Beauty, "Do not die and leave
me now! Until this moment I thought I felt only friendship
for you, but the pain I would endure if you died tells me that
I love you. Live, dear sweet Beast, and I'll be your wife!"

Suddenly, the night sky was filled with colored lights and shooting stars and music! Beauty, not knowing what to think, looked up for a second. But her concern for the Beast was so great that she turned back to him almost immediately. To her surprise, the Beast had vanished. In his place stood a handsome stranger dressed in royal finery.

"Where is the Beast?" demanded Beauty. "What have you done with him?"

"You are seeing him now," answered the stranger, kneeling down beside her. "I am a prince who once was stupidly unkind to a poor ugly old woman. She was a witch, who then put an enchantment on me because I had judged her only by her appearance. She made me as ugly as she was and condemned me to stay that way until a beautiful woman consented to marry me in spite of my ugliness. You alone in all the world were generous enough in heart to see beyond my outer self and love the goodness in my soul. Tell me, Beauty, will you still marry me? I do love you truly, and now I am free to offer you my crown as well as my heart."

Beauty looked deeply into the prince's eyes. She saw that they were the same eyes of her beloved Beast. As always, they were gentle and kind. But now instead of pain she saw joy and hope.

"Though you look different, I can see by your eyes that you are indeed my same dear Beast, whom I have come to love so much. Yes," she said, smiling. "If you are the same, then I will gladly marry you—this very day, this very hour, this very second!"

Together, Beauty and the prince walked back to the castle, where they found the woman in Beauty's dream waiting. This woman had magical powers, and she had transported Beauty's entire family there, too.

"I am the prince's fairy godmother," the woman said. "When the witch put her spell on him, I came to help him. But I was not allowed to guide you as I would have wished. All I could do was to help you take courage, so I appeared in your dream to comfort you.

"You have a wise heart, my child," continued the fairy godmother. "You loved the truest and best part of the Beast, rather than his appearance, and your choice will bring you happiness forever. Unlike your unfortunate sisters, who were not able to find what is important in someone, you looked into the eyes of the Beast and saw his soul. And I know you will be a great queen because your power will not change your goodness."

At that, the fairy plucked two roses—a red one for passion and a white one for purity of heart—and gave them to Beauty. As soon as Beauty touched them, the castle was transformed into the prince's kingdom. Beauty and the prince were married there in the grandest style and lived together afterward in well-deserved happiness.

The End